By Grand Central Station
I Sat Down and Wept

Elizabeth Smart was born in Ottawa, Canada, in 1913. She was educated at private schools in Canada and for a year at King's College, University of London. One day, while browsing in a London bookshop, she chanced upon a slim volume of poetry by George Barker – and fell passionately in love with him through the printed word. Eventually they communicated directly and, as a result of Barker's impecunious circumstances, Elizabeth Smart flew both him and his wife to the United States. Thus began one of the most extraordinary, intense and ultimately tragic love affairs of our time. They never married but Elizabeth bore George Barker four children and their relationship provided the impassioned inspiration for one of the most moving and immediate chronicles of a love affair ever written – *By Grand Central Station I Sat Down and Wept*. Originally published in 1945, this remarkable book is now widely recognized as a classic work of poetic prose which, more than four decades later, has retained all of its searing poignancy, beauty and power of impact.

After the war, Elizabeth Smart supported herself and her family with journalism and advertising work. In 1963 she became literary and associate editor of *Queen* magazine but subsequently dropped out of the literary scene to live quietly in a remote part of Suffolk. Elizabeth Smart died in 1986.

By the same author

ELIZABETH SMART

By Grand Central Station I Sat Down and Wept

Foreword by Brigid Brophy

PALADIN
GRAFTON BOOKS
A Division of the Collins Publishing Group

LONDON GLASGOW
TORONTO SYDNEY AUCKLAND

to Maximiliane von Upani Southwell

Paladin
Grafton Books
A Division of the Collins Publishing Group
8 Grafton Street, London W1X 3LA

Published in Paladin 1991

Previously published by Panther Books 1966
Reprinted 1970, 1978 (twice), 1980, 1984, 1985, 1986, 1987, 1988

First published in Great Britain by
Editions Poetry London (Nicholson & Watson) 1945

ISBN 0-586-09039-8

Printed and bound in Great Britain by
Collins, Glasgow

Set in Bembo

FOREWORD
by Brigid Brophy

I doubt if there are more than half a dozen masterpieces of poetic prose in the world. Onc of them, I am convinced, is Elizabeth Smart's *By Grand Central Station I Sat Down and Wept*, which was first published in 1945 – when, to the shame of those professing to practise criticism at the time, it made small stir and was left to create an underground reputation until, twenty-one years later, it has found a publisher wise enough to reissue it.

If poetic prose is the genre which can shew the fewest masterpieces, it is probably also the genre which can shew the longest list of truly and abysmally bad books – the sad, offensive litter left by writers who, in the excitement of discovering that it is unexpectedly easy to get up onto the heights, neglected to make provision for coming down again gracefully. For, as any love-letter-writer finds out, it is by no means as hard as you would guess to enrol your love, alongside that of Tristan and Isolde, among the eternal romances. The problem begins when you have to add the reminder that the money to pay the milk bill is under the vase on the sideboard.

Elizabeth Smart not merely solves the problem but turns it into artistic capital by taking the contrast between the intense and the banal as part of her actual subject. *By Grand Central Station* is largely *about* the astonishing dualism whereby a person can be a middle-class housewife and Isolde at the same time. 'I keep remembering,' says the heroine-narrator, 'that I am their host. So it is tomorrow's breakfast rather than the future's blood that dictates fatal forbearance.'

The danger to most poetic prose is that tomorrow's breakfast will intrude uninvited and thereby create bathos. In *By Grand Central Station*, the banal and material world is present in its own right. One great advantage this brings is that the book has no need to constitute an enclave without humour, as, for instance, Wagner's opera has to, lest a joke puncture the heroic proportions of Tristan and Isolde. Since it's firmly and irremediably *in* the book, the material world can be kicked sardonically about, fantasticated into a sick joke (the sentence of which I have already quoted part reads in full 'Like Macbeth, I keep remembering that I am their host') or chopped into savage hunks, as it is in the brilliant, agonizing passage where verses from *The Song of Songs* are spliced into the gross interrogations of a policeman.

The other great advantage is that the book can have a story. It is a genuine novel, as well as a rhapsody and a lament, though admittedly the story goes scarcely beyond the bare three lines of a love triangle, and even those have to be inferred from the narrator's rhapsodizing or lamentation over them. (I presume, for example, that it is for violating that extraordinary American law against crossing a state boundary with sexual purposes in mind that the lovers are arrested.)

Yet though the story is a narrow thread, it is a thread quite wiry enough to connect the book's moods and images. Baudelaire discovered no such thread on which to link his Little Poems in Prose, with the result that reading them is like picking through a box of marvellous but unstrung beads. The images in *By Grand Central Station* are individually beautiful but beautiful also in the order in which they are strung. Reading the book is like saying a tragic, pagan, erotic rosary.

And indeed the book's essential manner is liturgical. It is a chant. It demands to be read aloud, to be given concert performance. Like most poetic prose in English, it belongs to the tradition of the Authorized translation of works which in the original were presumably designed for some sort of performance, *The Song of Songs*, which it quotes to such piercing purpose, and the Psalms, from one of which it adapts its title. Its insistent rhythm, like theirs, is the rhythm of a throb. The entire book is a wound. Even when its rhythm expresses the throb of pleasure, the pleasure is so ardent that it lays waste the personality which experiences it.

In keeping with its tradition, *By Grand Central Station* is an exotic work. Its cadences make an outlandish howl. Its imagery is the plunder of diverse rituals and myths. Some of its similes are snatched from the furnishings of Catholicism: 'her thin breasts are pitiful like Virgin Shrines that have been robbed'. Some of its personifications have stalked out of the majestic classical myths, perhaps via the fatalistic pages of the Victorian masters of poetic prose, Walter Pater and Walter Savage Landor: 'Jupiter has been with Leda, and now nothing can avert the Trojan Wars.' Sometimes the classical personification is almost blotted out by a splurge of light-metaphor: 'but can I see the light of a match while burning in the arms of the sun?' – a metaphor ignited, I would guess, by Christopher Marlowe (himself a writer who never devised threads worthy of the brilliants he

9

had to string, so that he remains the great poet of isolated lines and couplets – which is how one knows that those scholars must be wrong who think he wrote the works of Shakespeare).

The mastery of *By Grand Central Station* is, of course, a mastery of metaphor – 'of course' because the pleasure we take in literature, and perhaps in any of the arts, seems ultimately always to lie in metaphor. For a reason I do not know (it may be too fundamental to be knowable), the human mind delights less in the exact evocation of one image, however beautiful, than in the lightning-flash (very like that of wit) which compares or actually fuses and assimilates two images, in the way that the very title of Elizabeth Smart's book assimilates Grand Central Station to the rivers of Babylon. This process goes, I believe, far beyond the verbal metaphors in the sentence-to-sentence texture of writing. I am fairly sure that when we say a book has 'depth' or 'universality' we mean that the author has implied perspectives viewed down which even the book's most seemingly single and particularized images, even its characters, are metaphors of something beyond themselves.

So it is apt enough that, in plundering classical mythology, *By Grand Central Station* repeatedly reaches towards the big family-tree of stories which recount how one image is palpably transformed, by magic, into another. 'O lucky Daphne, motionless and green to avoid the touch of a god. Lucky Syrinx, who chose a legend instead of too much blood!' The legends of Syrinx and Daphne are among those collected by Ovid under the title *Metamorphoses*, a word in which the *meta* is the same Greek preposition, signalling an act of

10

change, as in the word *metaphor*. A legend of metamorphosis is itself a metaphor of the very process of metaphor – of, that is, the very process of literary art.

The narrator's thoughts in *By Grand Central Station* run on metamorphosis (she is 'offended with my own flesh which cannot metamorphose into a printshop boy with armpits like chalices'); and in this the book remarkably resembles the work of the only other supreme prose-poet of our age, Jean Genet. (The resemblance must be quite spontaneous, since the two styles were formed in societies sealed off from one another by the war: the first version of Genet's *Notre-Dame des Fleurs* was published in France in 1943; *By Grand Central Station* appeared two years later in London and tells a story set, during the opening years of the war, in North America.) There are phrases in *By Grand Central Station* – 'No, my advocates, my angels with sadist eyes' – which might be by Genet in the excellent Frechtman translation. Like Elizabeth Smart, Genet is *par excellence* a metamorphic writer (one who can transform a man into a centaur in mid-sentence). Indeed, Genet, down to his very grammar, plays on the cardinal metamorphosis of 'he' into 'she'. Elizabeth Smart spins the same metaphor out of an allusion to another of Ovid's metamorphoses, the story of Hermaphroditus, the boy who went swimming and was so loved by the nymph who lived in the pool that her body fused with his and the two of them were transformed into one hermaphrodite. The reason the narrator of *By Grand Central Station* is offended that she cannot be transformed into a boy with (another Genet-like phrase) 'armpits like chalices' is that her lover is himself a metamorphic creature, who has fallen in love with just such a boy in a printshop; in one of the book's most inescapably memorable images, she sighs of her lover, 'Alas, I know he is the hermaphrodite whose love looks up through the appletree with a golden indeterminate face.'

Agreeing with Genet about the convertibility, the metamorphic indetermination, of the sexes, *By Grand Central Station* differs from him on the point of the convertibility of love and death. In Genet, the exchange runs in one direction only: pain becomes pleasure. Violence, criminality, murder itself are all metamorphosed into sexual acts; for Genet every weapon is phallic. In *By Grand Central Station* the exchange can go either way ('now the idea of dying violently becomes an act wrapped in attractive melancholy') but the book settles in the main for converting love and pleasure into torment. Genet is baroque and sensuous, his French tradition drawing deeper on Catholicism, his incantatory rhythms borrowed from invocations to the saints. *By Grand Central Station*, going back, through the English tradition, to the Authorized Version of the Old Testament, can in a just sense claim to be more *Jewish*. It is couched in the tone of exile, of (via Rilke) the psalmist's groan *de profundis*. 'Who, if I cried, would hear me among the angelic orders?' Even its martyrdoms are pre-Christian – half pagan, in fact, since they are many-eyed like Argos; and what they see with their many eyes is a vision not of heaven but of universal sorrow. Even a lover's hands inflict destruction. The phallos is always a weapon. 'I am shot with wounds which have eyes that see a world all sorrow . . . I am indeed and mortally pierced with the seeds of love.'

The myth of which *By Grand Central Station* most reminds me is indeed a pagan martyrdom – and one which many Old Masters gruesomely depicted as a sort of secular counterpart to their regular subject of the Crucifixion. This story, too, is told by Ovid in the *Metamorphoses*; and the painters were right to pick on it as aesthetics' answer to religion, since it is openly a story about art, being concerned with a music contest. The satyr Marsyas challenges Apollo to a competition. The god wins, of course, and punishes his opponent for daring to issue the challenge by skinning him alive. The tears of the satyr's friends are metamorphosed into a river, which is how the story comes to be in Ovid's collection. Concealed in this story, I have long felt, there is a conclusion the opposite to the one it tries to force on us. The point is that Apollo's art draws no one's perpetual tears ('perpetual' because a river flows for ever). At the time of the challenge and the contest, Marsyas was indeed the inferior musician. He did not become a great artist, with the power to move his audience in perpetuity, until his skin was removed. In the words of Patricia Highsmith, 'Writers and painters have by nature little in the way of protective shells and try all their lives to remove what they have' – even submitting to being flayed alive.

By Grand Central Station is one of the most shelled, skinned, nerve-exposed books ever written. It is a cry of complete vulnerability. To see it in the image of the flayed satyr is apt to its own imagery, since a satyr, a mixture of creatures, is himself an incarnate, a frozen, metamorphosis. It is also true to the moral of the myth, since the one metamorphosis whose magic truly works in real life is that whereby a gruesome and excruciating martyrdom can be transformed into a source of eternal pleasure, a work of art.

PART ONE

I am standing on a corner in Monterey, waiting for the bus to come in, and all the muscles of my will are holding my terror to face the moment I most desire. Apprehension and the summer afternoon keep drying my lips, prepared at ten-minute intervals all through the five-hour wait.

But then it is her eyes that come forward out of the vulgar disembarkers to reassure me that the bus has not disgorged disaster: her madonna eyes, soft as the newly-born, trusting as the untempted. And, for a moment, at that gaze, I am happy to forego my future, and postpone indefinitely the miracle hanging fire. Her eyes shower me with their innocence and surprise.

Was it for her, after all, for her whom I had never expected nor imagined, that there had been compounded such ruses of coincidence? Behind her he for whom I have waited so long, who has stalked so unbearably through my nightly dreams, fumbles with the tickets and the bags, and shuffles up to the event which too much anticipation has fingered to shreds.

For after all, it is all her. We sit in a café drinking coffee. He recounts their adventures and says, 'It was like this, wasn't it, darling?', 'I did well then, didn't I, dear heart?', and she smiles happily across the room with a confidence that appals.

How can she walk through the streets, so vulnerable, so unknowing, and not have people and dogs and perpetual calamity following her? But overhung with her vines of faith, she is protected from their gaze like the pools in Epping Forest. I see she can walk across the leering world and suffer injury only from the ones she loves. But I love her and her silence is propaganda for sainthood.

So we drive along the Californian coast singing together, and I entirely renounce him for only her peace of mind. The wild road winds round ledges manufactured from the mountains and cliffs. The Pacific in blue spasms reaches all its superlatives.

Why do I not jump off this cliff where I lie sickened by the moon? I know these days are offering me only murder for my future. It is not just the creeping fingers of the cold that dissuade me from action, and allow me to accept the hypocritical hope that there may be some solution. Like Macbeth, I keep remembering that I am their host. So it is tomorrow's breakfast rather than the future's blood that dictates fatal forbearance. Nature, perpetual whore, distracts with the immediate. Shifty-eyed with this fallacy, I plough back to my bed, up through the tickling grass.

So, through the summer days, we sit on the Californian coast, drinking coffee on the wooden steps of our cottages.

Up the canyon the redwoods and the thick leaf-hands of the castor-tree forbode disaster by their beauty, built on too grand a scale. The creek gushes over green boulders into pools no human ever uses, down canyons into the sea.

But poison oak grows over the path and over all the banks, and it is impossible even to go into the damp overhung valley without being poisoned. Later in the year it flushes scarlet, both warning of and recording fatality.

Between the canyons the hills slide steep and cropped to the cliffs that isolate the Pacific. They change from gold to silver, grow purple and massive from a distance, and disintegrate downhill in avalanches of sand.

Round the doorways double-size flowers grow without encouragement: lilies, nasturtiums in a bank down to the creek, roses, geraniums, fuchsias, bleeding-hearts, hydrangeas. The sea booms. The stream rushes loudly.

When the sea otters leave their playing under the cliff, the kelp in amorous coils appear to pin down the Pacific. There are rattlesnakes and widow-spiders and mists that rise from below. But the days leave the recollection of sun and flowers.

Day deceives, but at night no one is safe from hallucinations. The legends here are all of bloodfeuds and suicide, uncanny foresight and supernatural knowledge. Before the convict workers put in the road, loneliness drove women to jump into the sea. Tales were told of the convicts: how some went mad along the Coast, while others became hypnotized by it, and, when they were released, returned to marry local girls.

The long days seduce all thought away, and we lie like the lizards in the sun, postponing our lives indefinitely. But by the bathing pool, or on the sandhills of the beach, the Beginning lurks uncomfortably on the outskirts of the circle, like an unpopular person whom ignoring can keep away. The very silence, the very avoiding of any intimacy between us, when he, when he was only a word, was able to cause me sleepless nights and shivers of intimation, is the more dangerous.

Our seeming detachment gathers strength. I sit back impersonally and say, I see human vanity, or feel myself full of gladness because there is a gentleness between him and her, or even feel irritation because he lets her do too much of the work, sits lolling whilst she chops wood for the stove.

But he never passes anywhere near me without every drop of my blood springing to attention. My mind may reason that the tenseness only registers neutrality, but my heart knows no true neutrality was ever so full of passion. One day along the path he brushed my breast in passing, and I thought, Does this efflorescence offend him? And I went into the redwoods brooding and blushing with rage, to be stamped so obviously with femininity, and liable to humiliation worse than Venus' with Adonis, purely by reason of my accidental but flaunting sex.

Alas, I know he is the hermaphrodite whose love looks up through the appletree with a golden indeterminate face. While we drive along the road in the evening, talking as impersonally as a radio discussion, he tells me, 'A boy with green eyes and long lashes, whom I had never seen before, took me into the back of a printshop and made love to me, and for two weeks I went around remembering the numbers on bus conductors' hats.'

'One should love beings whatever their sex,' I reply, but withdraw into the dark with my obstreperous shape of shame, offended with my own flesh which cannot metamorphose into a printshop boy with armpits like chalices.

Then days go by without even this much exchange of metaphor, and my tongue seems to wither in my throat from the unhappy silence, and the moons that rise and set unused, and the suns that melt the Pacific uselessly, drive me to tears and my cliff of vigil at the end of the peninsula. I do not beckon to the Beginning, whose advent will surely strew our world with blood, but I weep for such a waste of life lying under my thumb.

His foreshortened face appears in profile on the car window like the irregular graph of my doom, merciless as a mathematician, leering accompaniment to all my good resolves. There is no medicinal to be obtained from the dried herbs of any natural hill, for when I tread those upward paths, the lowest vines conspire to abet my plot, and the poison oak thrusts its insinuation under my foot.

From the corner where the hill turns from the sea and goes into the secrecy and damp air of forbidden things, I stand disinterestedly examining the instruments and the pattern of my fate. It is a slow-motion process of the guillotine in action, and I see plainly that no miracle can avert the imminent deaths. I see, measuring the time, regarding equably the appearance, but I am as detached as the statistician is when he lists his thousands dead.

When his soft shadow, which yet in the night comes barbed with all the weapons of guilt, is cast up hugely on the pane, I watch it as from a loge in the theatre, the continually vibrating I in darkness. Swearing invulnerability, I measure mercilessly his shortcomings, and with luxurious scorn, ask who could be ensnared there.

But that huge shadow is more than my only moon, more even than my destruction: it has the innocent slipping advent of the next generation, which enters in one night of joy, and leaves a meadowful of lamenting milkmaids when its purpose is grown to fruit.

Also, smoothed away from all detail, I see, not the face of a lover to arouse my coquetry or defiance, but the gentle outline of a young girl. And this, though shocking, enables me to understand, and myself rise as virile as a cobra, out of my loge, to assume control.

He kissed my forehead driving along the coast in evening, and now, wherever I go, like the sword of Damocles, that greater never-to-be-given kiss hangs above my doomed head. He took my hand between the two shabby front seats of the Ford, and it was dark, and I was looking the other way, but now that hand casts everywhere an octopus shadow from which I can never escape. The tremendous gentleness of that moment smothers me under; all through the night it is centaurs hoofed and galloping over my heart: the poison has got into my blood. I stand on the edge of the cliff, but the future is already done.

It is written. Nothing can escape. Floating through the waves with seaweed in my hair, or being washed up battered on the inaccessible rocks, cannot undo the event to which there were never any alternatives. O lucky Daphne, motionless and green to avoid the touch of a god! Lucky Syrinx, who chose a legend instead of too much blood! For me there was no choice. There were no crossroads at all.

I am jealous of the hawk because he can get so far out of the world, or I follow with passionate envy the seagull swooping to possible cessation. The mourning-doves mercilessly coo my sentence in the woods. They are the hangmen pronouncing my sentence in the suitable language of love. I climb above the possessive clouds that squat over the sea, but the poison spreads. Naked I wait . . .

I am over-run, jungled in my bed, I am infested with a menagerie of desires: my heart is eaten by a dove, a cat scrambles in the cave of my sex, hounds in my head obey a whipmaster who cries nothing but havoc as the hours test my endurance with an accumulation of tortures. Who, if I cried, would hear me among the angelic orders?

I am far, far beyond that island of days where once, it seems, I watched a flower grow, and counted the steps of the sun, and fed, if my memory serves, the smiling animal at his appointed hour. I am shot with wounds which have eyes that see a world all sorrow, always to be, panoramic and unhealable, and mouths that hang unspeakable in the sky of blood.

How can I be kind? How can I find bird-relief in the nest-building of day-to-day? Necessity supplies no velvet wing with which to escape. I am indeed and mortally pierced with the seeds of love.

Then she leans over in the pool and her damp dark hair falls like sorrow, like mercy, like the mourning-weeds of pity. Sitting nymphlike in the pool in the late afternoon her pathetic slenderness is covered over with a love as gentle as trusting as tenacious as the birds who rebuild their continually violated nests. When she clasps her hands happily at a tune she likes, it is more moving than I can bear. She is the innocent who is always the offering. She is the goddess of all things which the vigour of living destroys. Why are her arms so empty?

In the night she moans with the voice of the stream below my window, searching for the child whose touch she once felt and can never forget: the child who obeyed the laws of life better than she. But by day she obeys the voice of love as the stricken obey their god, and she walks with the light step of hope which only the naïve and the saints know. Her shoulders have always the attitude of grieving, and her thin breasts are pitiful like Virgin Shrines that have been robbed.

How can I speak to her? How can I comfort her? How can I explain to her any more than I can to the flowers that I crush with my foot when I walk in the field? He also is bent towards her in an attitude of solicitude. Can he hear his own heart while he listens for the tenderness of her sensibilities? Is there a way at all to avoid offending the lamb of god?

Under the waterfall he surprised me bathing and gave me what I could no more refuse than the earth can refuse the rain. Then he kissed me and went down to his cottage.

Absolve me, I prayed, up through the cathedral redwoods, and forgive me if this is sin. But the new moss caressed me and the water over my feet and the ferns approved me with endearments: My darling, my darling, lie down with us now for you also are earth whom nothing but love can sow.

And I lay down on the redwood needles and seemed to flow down the canyon with the thunder and confusion of the stream, in a happiness which, like birth, can afford to ignore the blood and the tearing. For nature has no time for mourning, absorbed by the turning world, and will, no matter what devastation attacks her, fulfil in underground ritual, all her proper prophecy.

Gently the woodsorrel and the dove explained the confirmation and guided my return. When I came out of the woods onto the hill, I had pine needles in my hair for a bridalwreath, and the sea and the sky and the gold hills smiled benignly. Jupiter has been with Leda, I thought, and now nothing can avert the Trojan Wars. All legend will be born, but who will escape alive?

But what can the woodsorrel and the mourning-dove, who deal only with eternals, know of the thorny sociabilities of human living? Of how the pressure of the hours of waiting, silent and inactive, weigh upon the head with a physical force that suffocates? The simplest daily pleasantries are torture, and a samson effect is needed to avoid his glance that draws me like gravity.

For excuse, for our being together, we sit at the typewriter, pretending a necessary collaboration. He has a book to be typed, but the words I try to force out die on the air and dissolve into kisses whose chemicals are even more deadly if undelivered. My fingers cannot be martial at the touch of an instrument so much connected with him. The machine sits like a temple of love among the papers we never finish, and if I awake at night and see it outlined in the dark, I am electrified with memories of dangerous propinquity.

The frustrations of past postponement can no longer be restrained. They hang ripe to burst with the birth of any moment. The typewriter is guilty with love and flowery with shame, and to me it speaks so loudly I fear it will communicate its indecency to casual visitors.

How stationary life has become, and the hours impossibly elongated. When we sit on the gold grass of the cliff, the sun between us insists on a solution for which we search in vain, but whose urgency we feel unbearably. I never was in love with death before, nor felt grateful because the rocks below could promise certain death. But now the idea of dying violently becomes an act wrapped in attractive melancholy, and displayed with every blandishment. For there is no beauty in denying love, except perhaps by death, and towards love what way is there?

To deny love, and deceive it meanly by pretending that what is unconsummated remains eternal, or that love sublimated reaches highest to heavenly love, is repulsive, as the hypocrite's face is repulsive when placed too near the truth. Farther off from the centre of the world, of all worlds, I might be better fooled, but can I see the light of a match while burning in the arms of the sun?

No, my advocates, my angels with sadist eyes, this is the beginning of my life, or the end. So I lean affirmation across the café table, and surrender my fifty years away with an easy smile. But the surety of my love is not dismayed by any eventuality which prudence or pity can conjure up, and in the end all that we can do is to sit at the table over which our hands cross, listening to tunes from the wurlitzer, with love huge and simple between us, and nothing more to be said.

★　★　★

So hourly, at the slightest noise, I start, I stand ready to feel the roof cave in on my head, the thunder of God's punishment announcing the limit of his endurance.

She walks lightly, like the child whose dancing feet will touch off gigantic explosives. She knows nothing, but like autumn birds feels foreboding in the air. Her movements are nervous, there are draughts in every room, but less wise than the birds whom small signs send on three-thousand-mile flights, she only looks vaguely out to the Pacific, finding it strange that heaven has, after all, no Californian shore.

I have learned to smoke because I need something to hold on to. I dare not be without a cigarette in my hand. If I should be looking the other way when the hour of doom is struck, how shall I avoid being turned into stone unless I can remember something to do which will lead me back to the simplicity and safety of daily living?

IT is coming. The magnet of its imminent finger draws each hair of my body, the shudder of its approach disintegrates kisses, loses wishes on the disjointed air. The wet hands of the castor-tree at night brush me and I shriek, thinking that at last I am caught up with. The clouds move across the sky heavy and tubular. They gather and I am terror-struck to see them form a long black rainbow out of the mountain and disappear across the sea. The Thing is at hand. There is nothing to do but crouch and receive God's wrath.

PART TWO

God, come down out of the eucalyptus tree outside my window, and tell me who will drown in so much blood.

I saw her face coming out of the dying geraniums. It was angular with the tears that should have blurred her prolonged torture. Her body cringed, waiting for the wound which swung in perpetual suspension above her.

But her eyes pierced all the veils that protected my imagination against ruinous knowledge, to bleed me too in this catastrophic pool of birth.

Is there no other channel of my deliverance except by her martyrdom? At first my eyes reported what they saw but gave no meaning to the sight. I had no communication with misery. By severing all the wires of understanding I functioned like a normal being, and went about among devastation without seeing that it was there.

But who could be proof against that future ghost in the geraniums, holding pity like a time-bomb in its look of agony? What forgetfulness can nature devise, or what gangsters of justification can you, God, engage, to quiet this compassion which is the thief of my strength to endure?

On her mangledness I am spreading my amorous

sheets, but who will have any pride in the wedding red, seeping up between the thighs of love which rise like a colossus, but whose issue is only the cold semen of grief?

Not God, but bats and a spider who is weaving my guilt, keep the rendezvous with me, and shame copulates with every September housefly. My room echoes with the screams she never uttered, and under my floor the vines of remorse get ready to push up through the damp. The cricket drips remembrance unceasingly into my ear, lest I mislay any items of cruelty's fiendish inventory.

The trap is sprung, and I am in the trap.

But it is not to be eased from my pain which I crave when I pray God to understand my corrupt language and step down for a moment to sit on my broken bench. Will there be a birth from all this blood, or is death only exacting his greedy price? Is an infant struggling in the triangular womb?

I am blind, but blood, not love, blinded my eye. Love lifted the weapon and guided my crime, locked my limbs when, like a drowning man with the last lifeboat in sight, her anguish rose out of the sea to cry Help, and now over that piercing face superimposes the cloudy mask of my desire.

I have locked my door, but terror is ambushed outside. The eucalyptus batters the window, and I hear all smitten Europe wailing from the stream below. Malevolent ghosts appear at the black panes, unabashed by the pale crosses of the frame, for now Jesus Christ walks the waters of another planet, bleeding only history from his old wounds.

All cries are lost in the confusion of the storm. The coughing of sheep in the lost hills of Dorset, of gassed soldiers, of a two-year child with croup, roll into one avalanche of calamity, which sounds in the rushing of the stream, and which sounds even underneath the insensitive stomp that can break the whore's heart.

America, with Californian claws, clutches the Pacific, and now she masses her voices for frantic appeal. They roar like Niagara. They shake the synthetic hills. The sand of catastrophe is loosed and every breast is marked with doom.

But the cheating cicada arrives to lie All's Well in God's ear, which measures time so generously, and the woodlice are rocking their babies under the log. Anxiety lies still, while his eye makes its vast convolutions on remote and other worlds.

And then I force my vanity to stand on the cliff and let self contemplate self which only suicide can join.

Standing a thousand feet above the sea, how does my adoring reflection look now with the fishes of death swimming through its hair? Pearls and bubbles float up from the ocean bed, making a prettier noose for death, the last decoration of self-love, ring-a-rosing the gruesome vision. When we meet, and I clasp that deceiver in my arms, our amalgamation will poison the sea. But not tonight. There is no moon.

Threateners of life are horrible enough, and she whom I have injured, and whose agony it is my penalty to watch, lies gasping, but still living, on the land.

Shuddering like a coward, I dare not grasp either life or death from the ghoulish palm that offers them.

Under the redwood tree my grave was laid, and I beguiled my true love to lie down. The stream of our kiss put a waterway around the world, where love like a refugee sailed in the last ship. My hair made a shroud, and kept the coyotes at bay while we wrote our cyphers with anatomy. The winds boomed triumph, our spines seemed overburdened, and our bones groaned like old trees, but a smile like a cobweb was fastened across the mouth of the cave of fate.

Fear will be a terrible fox at my vitals under my tunic of behaviour.

Oh, canary, sing out in the thunderstorm, prove your yellow pride. Give me a reason for courage or a way to be brave. But nothing tangible comes to rescue my besieged sanity, and I cannot decipher the code of the eucalyptus thumping on my roof.

I am unnerved by the opponents of God, and God is out of earshot. I must spin good ghosts out of my hope to oppose the hordes at my window. If those who look in see me condescend to barricade the door, they will know too much and crowd in to overcome me.

The parchment philosopher has no traffic with the night, and no conception of the price of love. With smoky circles of thought he tries to combat the fog, and with anagrams to defeat anatomy. I posture in vain with his weapons, even though I am balmed with his nicotine herbs.

Moon, moon, rise in the sky to be a reminder of comfort and the hour when I was brave.

★ ★ ★

But the gentle flowers, able to die unceremoniously, remind me of her grief whose tears drown all ghosts, and though I swing in torture from the windiest hill, more angels weep for her whose devastated love runs into all the oceans of the world.

What did she cherish as her symbol, and how did she protect herself from panic when her ship pursued the month's-old storm, and she fought the cancer which was her knawing inward grief for her lost child? I have broken her heart like a robin's egg. Its wreck reaches her finite horizon.

What was your price, Gabriel, Michael of the ministering wing? What pulley from headlong man pulled you up in the nick of time, till you gushed vegetable laughter, and fed only off the sun? Was it your reward for wrestling successfully with such despair as this?

The texts are meaningless, they are the enemy's deception. My foot danced by mistake over the helpless, and bled no solace for my butchery. My hurt was not great enough to assuage my guilt. Tell me how to atone, dove in the eucalyptus, who speak with thunder of the future's revenge. Tell me this gush is the herald of my wonder.

My heart is its own destructive. It beats out the poisonous rhythm of the truth.

A wet wing brushes away the trembling night, and morning breathes cold analysis into my spectre-waiting mind. The vines assume their social airs, ingratiating green with children's fingers. The impotent eucalyptus stands gaunt.

But faint as hope, and definite as death, my possible phœnix of love is as bright as a totem-pole, in the morning, on the sky, breathing like a workman setting out on a job.

🌷 PART THREE

O the water of love that floods everything over, so that there is nothing the eye sees that is not covered in. There is no angle the world can assume which the love in my eye cannot make into a symbol of love. Even the precise geometry of his hand, when I gaze at it, dissolves me into water and I flow away in a flood of love.

Everything flows like the Mississippi over a devastated earth, which drinks unsurfeited, and augments the liquid with waterfalls of gratitude; which raises a sound of praise to deafen all doubters forever; to burst their shamed eardrums with the roar of proof, louder than bombs or screams or the inside ticking of remorse. Not all the poisonous tides of the blood I have spilt can influence these tidals of love.

But how can I go through the necessary daily motions, when such an intense fusion turns the world to water?

The overflow drenches all my implements of trivial intercourse. I stare incomprehension at the simplest question from a stranger, standing as if bewitched, half-smiling, like an idiot, feeling this fiery fluid spill out of my eyes.

I am possessed by love and have no options.

When the Ford rattles up to the door, five minutes (five years) late, and he walks across the lawn under the pepper-trees, I stand behind the gauze curtains, unable to move to meet him, or to speak, as I turn to liquid to invade his every orifice when he opens the door. More single-purposed than the new bird, all mouth with his one want, I close my eyes and tremble, anticipating the heaven of actual touch.

When we lie near the swimming pool in the sun, he comes through the bamboo bushes like land emerging from chaos. But I am the land, and he is the face upon the waters. He is the moon upon the tides, the dew, the rain, all seeds and all the honey of love. My bones are crushed like the bamboo-trees. I am the earth the plants grow through. But when they sprout I also will be a god.

And there is so much for me, I am suddenly so rich, and I have done nothing to deserve it, to be so overloaded. All after such a desert. All after I had learnt to say, I am nothing, and I deserve nothing.

The thick pines drop globular cones; the dishevelled palms, with their pantaloons falling down their trunks say,

It has happened, the miracle has arrived, everything begins today, everything you touch is born; the new moon attended by two enormous stars; the sunny day fading with a glow to exhilaration; all the paraphernalia of existence, all my sad companions of these last twenty years, the pots and pans in Mrs Wurtle's kitchen, ribbons of streets, wilted geraniums, thin children's legs, all the world solicits me with joy, leaps at me electrically, claiming its birth at last.

★   ★   ★

When we tear ourselves out of the night and come into the kitchen, Mrs Wurtle says, 'Romance, eh?', but she smiles, she turns away her head, and when we kiss behind her back as we help her dry the dishes, she says, 'Oh, you two love-birds, go on out again!'

What is going to happen? Nothing. For everything has happened. All time is now, and time can do no better. Nothing can ever be more now than now, and before this nothing was. There are no minor facts in life, there is only the one tremendous one.

We can include the world in our love, and no irritations can disrupt it, not even envy.

Mr Wurtle, sitting on the sofa late at night, says, with a legal air, 'Then I have it from you there is such a thing as Love?' I lean upon the cushion, faint from this few hours' separation, but I sigh, 'Yes, oh, yes,' and then, as if he were describing other worlds, diminutive, so petty I smother them in pity, he describes his intrigues, he bandies the Word that Was in the Beginning.

But the noise of my inside seas, the dazzle of this cataclysmic birth of love in me, cannot hear clearly what he says. To make a response is like rousing a heavy sleeper who longs to remain asleep. I smile, but I am in a trance, there is no reality but love.

I cannot hear beneath his subtle words the beginning of the world's antagonism: the hatred of the mediocre for all miracles. All I want is for everyone to go away and leave me a thousand lives in which to muse, only to muse, on this state of completion.

I was taunted so long. The meaning fluttered above my head, always out of reach. Now it has come to rest in me. It has pierced the very centre of the circle. I love,

love, love — , but he is also all things: the night, the resilient mornings, the tall poinsettias and hydrangeas, the lemon trees, the residential palms, the fruit and vegetables in gorgeous rows, the birds in the pepper-tree, the sun on the swimming pool.

There is no room for pity, of anything. In a bleeding heart I should find only exhilaration in the richness of the red.

Once I skulked wistfully through dim streets, aching after this unknown, hoping to pass by unnoticed in my drab dress and lopsided shoes with high heels, hoping, thus surreptitiously, to come upon it. But I was afraid, I was timid, and I did not believe, I hoped. I thought it would be like a bird in the hand, not a wild sea that treated me like flotsam.

But I have become a part of the earth: I am one of its waves flooding and leaping. I am the same tune now as the trees, hummingbirds, sky, fruits, vegetables in rows. I am all or any of these. I can metamorphose at will.

Do you need some joy or love? Are you sodden leaves in some forsaken yard? Are you deserted or cold or starved or paralysed or blind? Handfuls and handfuls for you, and to spare!

Make them up into bedsocks, teacosies, cushions against the cold, for their electricity is perpetual warmth, and can contaminate everything, and build at one touch a new and adorable world.

This is Today. This is where all roads strove to lead, all feet to attain. What are the world's problems and sorrows and errors? I am as at sea, and as ignorant and mystified, as the first day I ever saw algebra.

There are no problems, no sorrows or errors: they

join in the urging song that everything sings. This is the state of the angels, that spend their hours only singing the praises of the Lord. Just to lie savouring is enough life. Is enough.

Even in transient coffee-shops and hotels, or the gloom of taverns, the crooning of Bing Crosby out of a juke-box, and the bar-tender clanking glasses, achieve a perfect identity, a high round note of their own flavour, that makes me tearful with the gratitude of reception.

And merely his hand under those shabby tables, or guiding me across the stubble of the fields, makes my happiness as inexhaustible as the ocean, and as warm and comfortable as the womb.

When I saw a horde of cats gathering at a railway terminus to feed on a fish-head thrown near the tracks, I felt, It is the lavishness of my feelings that feeds even the waifs and strays. There are not too many bereaved or wounded but I can comfort them, and those 5,000,000 who never stop dragging their feet and bundles and babies with bloated bellies across Europe, are not too many or too benighted for me to say, Here's a world of hope, I can spare a whole world for each and every one, like a rich lady dispensing bags of candy at a poor children's Christmas feast.

I can compress the whole Mojave Desert into one word of inspiration, or call all America to obey my whim, like the waiter standing to take my order. I am delirious with power and invulnerability.

Take away what is supposed to be enviable: the silver brushes with my name, the long gown, the car, the hundred suitors, poise in a restaurant – I am still richer than the greediest heart could conceive, able to pour my overflowing benevolence over even the tight-mouthed look. Take everything I have, or could have, or anything the world could offer, I am still empress of a new-found land, that neither Columbus nor Cortez could have equalled, even in their instigating dream.

Set me as a seal upon thine heart, as a seal upon thine arm, for love is strong as death.

PART FOUR

But at the Arizona border they stopped us and said Turn Back, and I sat in a little room with barred windows while they typed.

What relation is this man to you? (My beloved is mine and I am his: he feedeth among the lilies.)

How long have you know him? (I am my beloved's and my beloved is mine: he feedeth among the lilies.)

Did you sleep in the same room? (Behold thou art fair, my love, behold thou art fair: thou hast dove's eyes.)

In the same bed? (Behold thou art fair, my beloved, yea pleasant, also our bed is green.)

Did intercourse take place? (I sat down under his shadow with great delight and his fruit was sweet to my taste.)

When did intercourse first take place? (The king hath brought me to the banqueting house and his banner over me was love.)

Were you intending to commit fornication in Arizona? (He shall lie all night betwixt my breasts.)

Behold thou art fair my beloved, behold thou art fair: thou hast dove's eyes.

Get away from there! cried the guard, as I wept by the crack of the door.

(My beloved is mine.)

Better not try any funny business, cried the guard, you're only making things tough for yourself.

(Let him kiss me with the kisses of his mouth.)

Stay put! cried the guard, and struck me.

They are taking me away in a police car. The policeman's wife sits stiffly in the front seat. They are prosecuting me for silence and for love.

The matron says: Give me your bracelet, no jewelry allowed. (My beloved – .) At once. And your ring. (My beloved – .) And your bag. Carrying all those outrageous cosmetics! Lipstick and perfume! No wonder you're where you are. (Stay me with flagons, comfort me with apples.)

The eyes of the jealous world peer through the peephole in the door, in the eyes of the keeper. But still the only torture is his absence.

The wall is scrawled with writing scratched with a pin: 'If you ever get out of here take my advice Be Good.'

Is he below my window with a serenade of tears?

When they parted us they watched me pressing against his knee, they intercepted our glances because of what was in our eyes.

What do you live for then?

I don't go for that sort of thing, the officer said, I'm a family man, I belong to the Rotary Club.

On the steps of the gaol we found a white bird. O my dove that art in the clefts of the rock in the secret places of the stair. It is the bird of liberty out in the cold, not official, not a bird with influence. Its heart beat against his thumb and he wept also, in the tele-phone box.

The inspector put it all down with six carbon copies. What a cad, he said, and the girl's a religious maniac.

When I thanked the gaolwoman for breakfast she said, Be quiet! It's not for you to talk.

The pepper-tree outside my barred window drooped with green love. Did they see such flagrant proof and still not believe? You are not allowed, said the woman, to open the window at the bottom.

Let this be a lesson, said the inspector, and Mr Wurtle said, You should have gone to different hotels, you should have lived in different countries, you should have been born in different epochs, in different worlds, then none of this would have happened.

Are all Americans chaste? All, by law. And every man hath his sword upon his thigh because of fear in the night. (By night on my bed I sought him whom my soul loveth.)

But then there's the rumble-seat of the car parked in a bend in the road? But no mountains of myrrh. No. And no hills of frankincense.

Get wise to yourself, Solomon, lay off all that stuff. Join a club. Get pally with the gang.

It is all written down. There are fourteen sheets and six copies of each. They fly over the continent like birds of ill omen, and will lie in files to blackball me from ease. Anyone who has pull can slip in and see what I said in the hour of my extremity and after ten hours' question-ing. The truth, the whole truth, and nothing but the truth, with Pontius Pilate leaning on the back of my chair, with thirty million cinema fans shouting sly advice, and love, oh, love, hungry in the Ford under the desert sun, blinding me and wounding me and tearing me apart.

Are you not convinced, inspector? Do you not believe in love?

He leered. Love? Eh, I've been around, you don't need to tell me.

But are all Americans virgin and faithful ever after? At parties, inspector, surely you know at parties?

You don't need to tell me, he said, I've been around.

But you, inspector, yourself?

I have no authority, he said, I'm only a cog in the machine, I have my duty to do.

But you care about justice, inspector, or you wouldn't be where you are?

I don't make the laws, he said, it isn't up to me, I have no authority. He smiled, but he was afraid of his smile and went away with a thin-lipped man and read the letters we had written.

They're only literary letters, I said, about things we both liked.

But you're a Communist? he said.

No.

But you've taken part in Communist activities?

No.

You have friends who are Communists?

Not more than other sorts.

He repented his smile and was severe in result. The thin-lipped man was livid with hate of our lineaments of gratified desire. He sneaked through the streets at dusk to warn the hotel.

The two policemen who had arrested us and brought us over the desert sat together on a bench, like minor schoolboys, washed and brushed and well-behaved, to return to their wives and calm households and their suppers, while we hurtled through confusion into tragedy because of their caprice on the Arizona border.

We're family men, they said, We don't go so much for love.

But what is important in life, what is it for? They looked down their noses. The thin-lipped man peered round the corner and noted down in his report: She tried to lure our men.

You may say Goodbye, said the inspector who had smiled, but wedged his lever of speculation between our mouths. (Milk and honey are under your tongue.) Let this be a lesson, he said.

When I wept, when I wept at last loudly, they showed their satisfaction, all five, and rubbed their hands, and their two-days' work was done.

My love, my dove, my undefiled, go into the telephone box with Diogenes and dial a number that someone will understand. It was income tax that did in Al Capone. What is the issue now?

O his lost look in the desert town crossing the street alone, with his shoulders stooped, as they drove me away in the police car. This cannot, cannot be true, I thought. For too much love, only for too much love.

Who is for us if these are so fiercely against? All our wishes were private, we desired no more scope than ourselves. Could we corrupt the young by gazing into each other's eyes? Would they leave their offices? Would big business suffer?

'You antagonized them,' said Mr Wurtle. 'You behaved stupidly. None of that need have happened.

You should have buttered them up, jollied them along. You shouldn't have talked so much.'

'But they made me swear – .'

'A formality.'

'But they brought in the nature of Truth – .'

'What is truth?' said Mr Wurtle. 'Those federal boys are tough.'

PART FIVE

And so, returning to Canada through the fall sunshine, I look homeward now and melt, for though I am crowned and anointed with love and have obtained from life all I asked, what am I as I enter my parents' house but another prodigal daughter? I see their faces at which I shall never be free to look dispassionately. They gaze out of the window with eyes harassed by what they continually fear they see, like premature ghosts, straggling homeward over the plain.

And I, who have the world in my pocket, can bring them nothing to comfort their disappointment or reward their optimism, but supplicate again for the fatted calf which they killed so often before and so in vain. Parents' imaginations build frameworks out of their own hopes and regrets into which children seldom grow, but instead, contrary as trees, lean sideways out of the architecture, blown by a fatal wind their parents never envisaged.

But the old gold of the October trees, the stunted cedars, the horizons, the chilly gullies with their red willow whips, intoxicate me and confirm belief in what I have done, claiming me like an indisputable mother saying Whether or No, Whether or No, my darling. The great rocks rise up to insist on belief, since they remain though Babylon is fallen, being moulded, but never conquered, by time pouring from eternity. Can I expect less than sympathy from those who see such things when they draw aside their curtains in the mornings? Like Antæus, when I am thrust against this earth, I bounce back recharged with hope. Every yellow or scarlet leaf hangs like a flag waving me on. The brown ones lie on the ground like a thousand thousand witnesses to the simplicity of truth.

So love may blind the expectations in my parents' eyes; or eloquence rise from my urgency and melt them too with ruth; understanding may now stalk down Sparks Street in every clerk, undoing wrongs begun before Wolfe; or in Honey Dew cafés a kind look glance towards me as I open the door.

Asking no one's forgiveness for sins I refuse to recognize, why do I cry then to be returning homeward through a land I love like a lover? From a long way off those faces with their prayers like wounds peer out of the window, stiff with anxiety, but ready to welcome me with love. The sound of their steps pacing before the fireplace voices all the pain of the turning world.

O Absalom, Absalom, melt, melt with ruth.

Coming from California, which is oblivious of regret, approaching November whips me with the passion of the dying year. And after the greed already hardening part of the American face into stone, I fancy I see kindness and gentleness looking out at me from train windows. Surely the porter carrying my bags has extracted a spiritual lesson from his hardship. Surely this acceptance of a mediocre role gives human dignity.

And over the fading wooden houses I sense the reminiscences of the pioneers' passion, and the determination of early statesmen who were mild but individual, and able to allude to Shakespeare while discussing politics under the elms. No great neon face has been superimposed over their minor but memorable history. Nor has the blood of the early settlers, spilt in feud and heroism, yet been bottled by a Coca-Cola firm and sold as ten-cent tradition.

The faces, the faded houses, the autumn air, everything is omens of promise to the prodigal. But leaning against the train window, drunk with the hope which anything so unbegun always instils, I remember my past returnings: keep that vision, I pray, pressing my forehead against the panes: the faces *are* kind; the people *have* reserve; the birds gather in groups to migrate, forecasting fatal change: remember, when your eyes shrivel aggrievedly because you notice the jealousy of those that stay at home, here is no underlining of an accidental picturesqueness, but a waiting, unself-conscious as the unborn's, for future history to be performed upon it.

Remember that although this initial intoxication disappears, yet these things in that hour moved you to tears, and made of an outward gaze through the dining-car window a plenitude not to be borne.

PART SIX

As I sat down in the swivel chair in my father's office, with his desk massively symbolic between us, I realized that I could never defend myself. What was my defence but one small word which I dared not utter, because jazz singers and hypocritical preachers and Dorothy Dix had so maligned it.

'Love? Stuff and nonsense!' my mother would say, 'It's loyalty and decency and common standards of behaviour that count.' But her eyes were like medieval wildmen in her head, clutching at her diminishing days that brought them no rest.

But from my father I had hoped for more. He could spread his mind out before you like the evidence of a case. But if he saw emotion approaching he smiled painfully, rocking in his swivel chair, hoping it would pass: 'Aren't you just a little obsessed about this thing?'

And then the whole parade of unbelievers filed past: the leering police thugs, the insinuations of Mr Wurtle and his conversational pin-pricks – 'Then I have it from you there is such a thing as Love?' – the well-meaning matrons who, from their insulated living say, 'My dear, I think you would regret it afterwards if you broke up a marriage,' 'When you felt it about to happen the right thing would have been to have gone away at once,' and always battalions of blindmen carrying placards of public vote: 'If he needs money why doesn't he get a job?' 'What does he know of Love that lets his country down in her Hour-of-Need?'

Dear God, how sympathetic the frozen Chaudiere Falls seem under the December sky, compared with these inflexible faces. Even the snow is protection for the next generation, which sleeps. They, who talk of a greater love, what is underneath the long cold of their look? They warm no bud of humanity under their semblance, for it is no semblance.

I am the green leprechaun of legends, knocking at the houses asking for bread to find out who is kind. All are wanting, though, none are kind. 'I am saving my money for the Red Cross. What War-work are you doing, my dear?'

Go, my little brother, so that more and better blood may flow to be mopped up with floppy consciences. He has his hair cropped off like a convict and joins jokingly in bloodthirsty games: 'I've never met this guy, but he sounds to me like a cad.'

Did you know that 11,000 faces identical with Christ's are growing thinner in the federal prison? They had no money and no guns, and their trousers were not creased. The policeman grows fatter each day and rivals the new tanks. He blots out the doorway of the little café. A couple seeing him spills the milk at the counter, remembering what they did under the bridge last night.

But the policeman is blind. He strikes only when he hears a loud noise. There are others, though, who have eyes like shifty hawks, and they prowl the streets searching for a face whereon an illegal kiss might be forming.

No, there is no defence for love, and tears will only

increase the crime. Be reasonable. Be usual. You're a clever girl. You've got brains. Get busy and make something of yourself.

So there are to be no obsequies. There is to be no mention of that which was to have conquered the world, and after the world, death. Not one of all those martyrs nailed to every tree in the western hemisphere will find favour in the editor's measuring eye. On the amusement page, to fill up space, one inch and a half, perhaps, of those who were forced to die. Butter is up ten cents. The human being is down.

Remember Ottawa on New Year's Eve sulking under snow, and you with quinzy cutting your new year's wishes in two.

My mother said, No! I want nothing more to do with you! as I put out my hand to say goodbye; and my father, over the phone, said, Let me know where you are, weary and curt; you said, out of your bruised throat, Don't have reactions against me because I spit phlegm. *You* did me most injustice.

Where were we going then? Anywhere to be together and alone. Such a wish offends all people who have less than love in their pockets. Besides, it's time here to put on uniforms, not nightgowns. It is no use asking them what good I would be, who, without you, become a corpse, a deadweight: questioned in court one must fish haphazardly for the answers they want. The very word Love offends with its nudity. It stopped being practical when the most expensive camel stuck in the needle's eye.

When I left Ottawa I said, Whom shall I say goodbye to? but could think of no one. Some greet me with genuine smiles, but years of my absence pass without their notice, and my conversation to them seems protestation.

Do I delight in shocking my elders? Don't I care to win the War?

There have been men who have been more remembered than nations, and nations of men have been willing to die for a word.

Then my word or your word?

Don't be impudent, child.

There is my sister at home with sons for hostage, fighting for one week free to win a job. Then there is my aunt like a harpy of relentlessness, fighting to get all women into uniform.

Who dares breathe pleasure when war is the word but not yet the actuality? Here the gossip of war covers over the goal which might in small degrees even be present now. In London they know this better, and strangers kiss in underground shelters or find jokes in bombed effigies.

Be at hypocrisy's funeral, O my dear country, and pay the usual hypocritical tear. Mine I am saving for quite another event.

Which event, if you, my dearest, by now shall have proved to be other than I hope it to be, will have a burial by salt sea tear more memorable than the Roumanian debris, and a one-woman battle as bloody as ten million men's. For I was raised for this event from more than a three-day burial, and would have built memorials to last longer than 2,000 years. From this conjunction of impossibles might have arisen a generation whose eyes knew how to appraise such meteors and carry a legend like a banner before them.

Not that I wish to blaspheme, or to say, See what I am. I wish only to say, Remember Ottawa on New Year's Eve: on that day which so threatened and whose antagonists it was not nothing to have said Pooh to, I did choose without influence or fanfare or any signpost to point me anywhere but away from you.

Neither reason nor sense nor greed nor pity nor perspicacity nor worldly wisdom nor expediency nor filial duty gave my hand into yours. No one can say I was carried away in that hour.

So I say now, for the record of my own self, and to remember when I may be other than I am now: In spite of everything so strong in dissuasion, so rampant in disapproval, I saw then that there was nothing else anywhere but this one thing; that neither nunneries nor Pacific Islands nor jungles nor all the jazz of America nor the frenzy of warzones could hide any corner which housed an ounce of consolation if this failed. In all states of being, in all worlds, this is all there is.

Remember also that I said, Though this is all there is, though it is the one and vulnerable, mortal to all attack, a poverty-stricken word against the highly-financed world, yet it is not meagre, it is enough. I do not accept it sadly or ruefully or wistfully or in despair. I accept it without tomorrows and without any lilies of promise. It is the enough, the now, and though it comes without anything, it gives me everything.

With it I can repopulate all the world. I can bring forth new worlds in underground shelters while the bombs are dropping above; I can do it in lifeboats as the ship goes down; I can do it in prisons without the guard's permission; and O, when I do it quietly in the lobby while the conference is going on, a lot of states-men will emerge twirling their moustaches, and see the birth-blood, and know that they have been foiled.

Love is strong as death.

So tonight we will put the whole untidy world into a nest, and it will hang swinging comfortably as if it were as far away and as glossed over by history as the Red Indian's right to be free.

Whether or not your quinzy controls all our thoughts and actions, the night will be lined with silk and surrounded by hours of peace, ghostless and luxurious. It will be a sleep that is a sleep, not just an ether to dispose of twelve more useless hours, sleep that will be its own end, not a waiting for the passing of time: THE time.

I shall be able now, whether or not you make me weep, to include the landscape as I hurry home, and be influenced by the meanest birch or pine; or a triangle of light may teach me as I zip my yellow tunic at the morning window.

Why should I be so paradoxically showered on now by the incidentals of delight, now when I am most rich and most invulnerable? I could have used them so well, even one of them, I could have made them into a great sign, when I was taking streetcars to and from my mother's house, with every sense desolated; when not to have you was alone too much taste of hell. Then my mother's clutch held me every way, with claws of biology and pity and hysterical hypnotism, and made me long for my annihilation. Can even Freud explain the terror of that clutch, the inescapability of its greed for authority, and why it was stronger than the North East wind, memory, reason, or Pre-Cambrian rock?

No, for it is outside category and explanation, and lies in the footnote that admits phenomena and disturbing fact, but has no answer to why certain angels have haloes of singing birds, or why Balder had mistletoe growing out of his heel.

But as long as the accessories are such now as to make me over-armed with weapons to combat the antagonistic world, even if a thousand programs go wrong, I won't lament that past I was when I could see no future. You may be an invalid for life, or paralytic, or leprous, we may starve in gutters, or follow the plague, I shall still have a pocketful of rye, whose currency no Foreign Exchange can control, nor value be diminished by transplantation.

Remember also, when you hold your so vulnerable head between your hands, that what we are being punished for, and worse, what we are punishing for, is not just that sea of peace we achieve when you call me You Bitch, but the Cause. (The cause, my soul.)

For sometimes when this aspect, the warmth that swoons, has such a rich retinue, we say, We are too happy, we are too rich and strong. And then, overcome by guilt or shame to be so favoured, we waver and say, It is unfair that the weak and the unlucky ones suffer and we don't.

But if you do me the wrong of thinking I am beautiful, that I have a million rescuers from despair, and therefore I can take calamity better than anyone else, remember, truly, it is only you who bestow even these gifts upon me. Therefore, how much greater my loss must be which takes away even what appears to be mine by nature, my power to endure and resist.

Remember I am not temptation to you, but everything is which inclines you away. Nor are you to me, but my entire goal. Sometimes you see this as clearly as I do now, for you say, 'Do you think if I didn't I could have . . .?'

But Pity like a beggar-child sidles up to you with beseeching palm and eyes more moving than beauty. And walking down Third Avenue you hear the mice squeak in the housewives' traps.

Do you see me then as the too-successful one, like a colossus whose smug thighs rise obliviously out of sorrow? Or as the detestable all-female, who grabs and devours, invulnerable with greed?

Alas, these thoughts are your sins, your garments of shame, and not the blond-sapling boys with blue eyeshadow leaning amorously towards you in the printshop.

There are some who love Lucifer because he lost the battle with God. The devil had some justice on his side, and perhaps something was rotten in the state of heaven then. Don't think I haven't seen chipmunks' tails abandoned on logs to save their lives, nor gnawed rabbits' paws in traps mixed up with the steel.

When I hurry down the street it is not any game I hold in my mind and play with the passers by, but the shyness which keeps seamstresses nervously peering out of their badly-lit rooms, half hidden behind the drab lace, preferring to dream over their gas-jets and mild tea than submit to the rude investigations of the world. There are such, you know, and they treat their possessions gently, as if they were children or animals. But don't think they are overlooked. Thousands of angels yearn over them, are even now embroidering them skirts, and getting ready to teach them the rumba.

Who weeps for the angels, though, or notices when they turn aside to stiffen their upper lips?

Not that I claim to be an angel, too. But I know that to be even gently bright and happy raises enemies.

Only remember: I am not the ease, but the end.

I am not to blind you but to find you.

What you think is the sirens singing to lure you to your doom is only the voice of the inevitable, welcoming you after so long a wait. I was made only for you.

Eons have been evolving and planets disintegrating and forming to compel these two together. If this enormous conspiracy of your watching fates fails, don't you see how I will be blamed?

Oh, it will be no use to show them your son and say, Look, I salvaged this from the blood. Don't you know how weary they are of procrastination? You are the hour and the generation that they marked for result.

And also, your son does not step down out of his hammock to be anyone's scapegoat, but to collect his own apple with his own sin, as his son, too, will do at the proper time.

 **PART SEVEN**

They have hung that marvellous face branded with numero-logical shame in the criminal's gallery. He is straitjacketed to the bed. Is it a hospital or gaol? I can't tell. I am shut out. I ran down all the rubber corridors, but the seats in the theatre were empty.

No. I am confused.

He said No Visitors were allowed. Not even on Friday.

Then I went with magazines and fruit, and the nurse said, Go along in, his wife is there.

So I turned back, but in the corridor every door was locked. No, some were glass, but double, and it was snowing outside.

My love, my dearest love, where are you? Under the greenwood tree. Yes. (Also our bed is green. And the smell of his nose like apples.)

The stairs were spiral and went down for miles. But carpeted. O, yes, but people were watching meanly and commenting on my shabby clothes. The whirlwind was just above, with fearful claws, not wind, you know, no, but small bits of newspaper, whirling dangerously near. I am afraid. Suppose it caught me up?

It was about this time that I found the letter folded: My dearest love, It is all you: I want to go on as I have before. I put it back, yes. But he took it from the marble fireplace and threw it away. I saw him. The tree outside the window was weighted with snow. This proves it, doesn't it?

At ten minutes to midnight he said, Go out and get me a thermos bottle, and I heard the New Year come in as I waited by the drugstore counter. The snow melted and the streets were slushy with blood.

I meant to tell you about The Child. It was always like that. The room was ankle-deep in blood.

Yes, I know.

I heard her wail: Why didn't you let me keep the child, O why didn't you let me keep the child?

It was a little girl, dark, with long fingers. She was pretty, wasn't she?, not at all like most little babies.

The man at the beer parlour said, You've bought nothing for an hour, I'm afraid I must ask you to leave. The clothes were steaming on the coils, still wet. It is December, and the woods are rather wet for a rendezvous. If you sit on the stones you get piles. Why do so many telegrams arrive? Shall we send another?

Yes, it's only humane.

You'd hate me if I acted otherwise, wouldn't you?

When he came out of gaol his eyes were dead and he said, I have lost my innocence, staring at the ceiling and chewing a frightful drug.

When he came out of the hospital he had a bandage round his throat. They had to tie him down, he railed so. The anæsthetist was an artist, he had armpits just like chalices, just to see a top hat gave him an erection, he'd have no trouble getting into the army.

I've done this twice before, today, he said as we lay

in the orchard, once with her, once with you, and once with the jaw-bone of an ass. One, two, three.

My love, I think I see a little blood on your clothes.

Yes, that's from the belly of the whale.

Women are so possessive.

As the apple-tree among the trees of the wood, so is my beloved. Every furrow in the orchard is ploughed except at the trunk of the tree where the grass grows. There it stands up like the Golden Fleece.

Forgive me, for, of course, I am serving two.

Could you tell me the way out of here, please, doctor, or inspector, I can't quite see who you are in this light.

No one hears me. It's the silent rubber floor. I've been hours and hours knocking on the various doors.

But you're a Communist?

No.

A Pacifist?

No.

A Cad? In your case, then, I think the only thing for you to do is to go to the edge of a cliff and say, Here goes Nothing, and jump. That will be eighty-eight dollars and two dollars more for the medicine.

My love, why did you leave me on Lexington Avenue in the Ford that had no brakes?

It stalled in the traffic and broke down outside her window. She was writing a letter: I love you very much: Careful Now in capitals.

That was a different letter.

Yes, but I get confused. One day she saw a golden oriel in the orchard. One day she said, Then have your orgy with Blondie, work out your passion on her.

I see it all, the poop of burnished gold. If I got angry and made a scene?

But No. No.

No. I believe you, of course, I believe you, for didn't you say I was the one? Yes, you said, Take care of this girl for she is what makes my blood circulate and all the stars revolve and the seasons return.

This was my dream, and why I had circles under my eyes this morning at breakfast. Everyone noticed it, and I think one of them sniggered.

You don't take much interest in politics, do you? You never read the newspapers? I drank my coffee, but I had a slight feeling of nausea. It's to be expected, I don't mind it at all, it's nothing.

My love, are you feeling better?

He can't talk, he can only mutter.

O my dear, O my dear, drink a little milk, lie down and rest a little. I will comfort you. I can carry love like Saint Christopher. It is heavy, but I can carry it. It's the stones of suspicion I stumble on. Did I say suspicion? No.

No. No. It's nothing. I love you. A slight feeling of nausea, that's all.

After a while I got out into the open air, and his face was the moon hanging in the snowy branches.

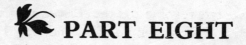

PART EIGHT

His brother and his mother and his grandmother lie abandoned in death on the stones of the London Underground. Two antagonists, squeezed in the smallest possible space, prop each other to sleep.

Letters blackly scarred with the censor's knife translate the unimaginable: 'I heard a child ask where its legs were.' 'We think with longing now of onions and lemons.' The radio voice says: 'Out of privation and the death of friends arises a new determination.'

Bombs are bigger, but the human brains they burst remain the same. It is the faces we once kissed that are being smashed in the English coastal towns, the hands we shook that are swept up with the debris; the headlines speak to us of our private lives: yet still the mangy dog skulking under our window arouses a realer pity. Babylon and Sodom and the Roman Empire fell, but the winter blizzard cuts as cruelly as ever, and love still uproots the heart better than an imagined landmine.

His brother and his mother and his grandmother lie buried, but in the lava of history. They are already wept for by posterity's tragic chorus. Their effigies will arise when a new Pompeii is opened.

But this bleeding minute cares only for the moment's fact which says that it is near dawn and that he has not come back: is not consoled because eight hours ago on the phone his trembling voice announced their deaths.

Why should even ten centuries of the world's woe lessen the fact that I love? Cradle the seed, cradle the seed, even in the volcano's mouth. I am the last pregnant woman in a desolated world. The bed is cold and jealousy is cruel as the grave.

When my eyes float around the room like two ships lost on the sea, I know the exact measurements of my captivity. For I cannot escape by bashing my head against the box-like confine, nor can I summon into my company ghosts with visionary eyeballs. There is never anywhere to cry. The walls are always too thin and the sobs so loud that they echo down the street and across salt water bays.

There is never and nowhere a time for such a word.

For clues to all calamity I have the painful lovemaking of alley-cats along the roofs outside my window; the quarter-hour chiming of a clock whose notes partly never strike; the wheezing of the coils, cheerful and regular like crickets. The elevator, though, clatters a promise of event never fulfilled, and sometimes the plumbing shrieks remotely like the message of a falling comet.

I review all I know, but can synthesize no meaning. When I doze, the Fact, the certain accomplished calamity, wakes me roughly like a brutal nurse. I see it crouching inflexibly in a corner of the ceiling. It comes down in geometrical diagonal like lightning.

It says, I remain, I AM, I shall never cease to be: your memory will grow a deathly glaze: you will forget, you will fade out, but I cannot be undone.

Thus every quarter-hour it puts the taste of death in my mouth, and shows me, but not gently, how I go whoring after oblivion.

The wallpaper drips gloom, and the walls press in like dread. This dark hotel room is the centre of the whirl-pool where no one can any longer resist.

Here is the bed where love so often liberated us and dissolved the walls, but where also the night shook him by the collar like a dog till he spat out the rag ends of his fear: 'You're a cunt! You're nothing but a cunt!'

'You know you're only trying to bribe me!'

'No! No! No!'

Over there is the chair, less lucky in function, where he read the newspaper or waited impersonally absorbed. It is my worst antagonist for most often it won him away. Though sometimes it opened benignly and I saw him through his fingers beaming the possessive while I strutted for him.

The mirror is the best breeder. On lucky nights it returned me my face as if it were bestowing a proud honour: this is the face that launched a thousand nights of love. This is the trap that lured the archangel into your bed: this is the precarious instrument that pulls polestars to you.

But sometimes, alone, it caught my two eyes like butterflies on pins, and showed me a face about to be submerged by tears, hounded back to the sterility of its own counsel, when the day of wrath, now avalanching into the present, should arrive.

The sight of that mad face in the half-lit room drove me to prayers and loud noise. Your own shadow meeting you announces the end. A too likely and too imminent feature gnawed that face to death. But then the electric light burned out, and the bleak dawn showed only enlarged pores and the remnants of yesterday's cosmetics.

But again and again when I peer into the mirror to find a distortion of my own image which would make my pain into a bearable legend, that form bends over me in embrace forever, like the persistent neon lights, or I remember the night it turned him into an Assyrian girl, casting down his lashes under a blossoming turban. Then we were two sisters and I the protive. He had no breasts, and this was nostalgic. O the glittering incest bird. But all so gracefully submissive, who will put the hand over the heart? He removed his head-dress and we were plain people ready for the night.

The typewriter typed holes in our foolproof games, and made the gap that nearly broke us as well as my fingernails. I see now how alien love is also to the clerical, and why girls can be so practical and still never fulfilled. It gnaws down to the scaffolding, which has never heard of the wish for a pink ruffled negligee nor the leisure to concoct new ways to indulge the languorous and voluptuous five senses. It drills nerves, and its sympathy is with the miser. It is not an instrument of love.

In cafés, behind plush curtains, where for twenty-five cents each we had temporary luxury, sometimes things went well, and I held my breath and poised my fork above the fishcakes when revelation came. Glancing sideways into the mirror, I could see his face watching me, and had no doubt then of his indulgence.

The pawnshop and the bank, where we went for letters and answers to our appeals for rescue, had different moods, like players subject to revolving coloured lights. But neither the shabby streets nor the cooped-up hotel ever became for me, as they were always for him, symbols of wretchedness and no cash, or a land where there is no one to talk to and nothing ever happens.

Wherever we went, though, whatever we did, we had always to return like cornered foxes to the hotel room. And always the wallpaper dispersed with its heavy writing any optimism we might have gathered. There were no solutions in the writing on the wall. It urged us to despair. It is criminally responsible for all histories.

For who plans suicide sitting in the sun? It is the pile of dust under the bed, the dirty sheets that were never washed, that precipitate fatal action.

When the ship cracks in the typhoon, we cover our heads and tell ourselves that all will resolve back to normal. But we are unbelieving. This time may not be like the other times that with time grew into cheerful anecdotes. The stories we heard, about the ten thousand buried in the quake, were, after all, true.

And more irredeemable than any human catastrophe, the dinosaurs trailed across the desert to their end. They left no descendants to embellish their saga, but only the white bones and the marks in the clay for archeologists to make into footnotes. Our hour may be this hour, and our end the dinosaurs'.

So perhaps there will be no revolving back at all, and only archives, full of archetypes, like the composite photographs of movie heroines.

But with or without us, the Day itself must return,

we insist, when the Joke at least sits basking in the sun, decorating her idle body with nameless red, once blood.

Philosophy, like lichens, takes centuries to grow and is always ignored in the Book of Instructions. If you can't Take It, Get Out.

I can't take it, so I lie on the hotel bed dissolving into chemicals whose adventure will pursue time to her extinguishment, without the slightest influence from these few years when I held them together in human passion.

O where does he stalk like a horse in pastures very far afield? I cannot hear him, and silence writes more terrible things than he can ever deny. Is there a suspicion the battle is lost?

Certainly he killed me fourteen nights in succession. To rise again from such slaughter Messiah must indeed become a woman. He said this absence was the mere mechanics of the thing. But It is not the same.

He did the one sin which Love will not allow. The police, domestic scenes, cooling friends, the bribed provincial cops, the sordidness of hotels, were powerless, but love has other laws, whose infringement, even by a slight trespass, is punished without trial.

He did sin against love, and though he says it was in Pity's name, and that Pity was only fighting a losing battle with Love, he was useless to Pity, and in wavering, injured Love, which was, after all, what he staked all for, all he had, ungamblable.

So I am caught without a polestar. What inhibition can restrain my despair? What can pull me back?

Too many nights have built their explosive facts, and without the one Fact which these facts invalidate, the

5,000,000 refugees, the corpses that died of starvation, the blood and the mangling, have absolutely no dam. 'Only Love can with a great gaze stop.'

But where is Love? Crucified over 500 miles. Stretched out in the snow over the dilapidated country where only the birds are at home, and they only for six months of the year.

How can I put love up to my hopes so suicidal and wild-eyed when the matter is too simple and too plain: it is *her* tears he feels trickling over his breast each night; it is for *her* he feels the concern; and the *pity* after all, not the love, fills all his twenty-four hours.

Perhaps I am his hope. But then she is his present. And if then she is his present, I am not his present. Therefore, I am not, and I wonder why no one has noticed I am dead and taken the trouble to bury me. For I am utterly collapsed. I lounge with glazed eyes, or weep tears of sheer weakness.

All people seem criminally irrelevant. I ignore everyone and everything, and, if crossed or interrupted in my decay, hate. Nature is only the irking weather and flowers crude reminders of stale states of being.

I have not been in love but in despair these last ten days. And without love I am lost more fatally than he can have any idea of, who thinks nature revives me so resiliently. Nature has been good, and she has worked miracles upon me and for me, but this is where it all leads, and for what she preserved me. So if it lacks totality, it topples, it lacks all, and I am as dead as the parson's egg was bad.

Sometimes, when I squeeze the pain from side to side in my caged head, I say: If I am suffering, think what she suffered – a hundred times more and without hope, and I was dazzlingly happy on top of her profound and excruciating misery.

Then her hair, falling like grief, floats in the deserted park, lifted with every dead leaf the wind disturbs; or her gesture that stumbled with too many meanings to stroke his temple with the back of her hand.

But it is not for her my heart opens and breaks: I die again and again only for myself. For her moving image prevents even my cry to him for help. For even if he loves me, he is in her arms.

O the fact, the unalterable fact: it is she he is with: he is with her: he is not with me because he is sleeping with her.

But I do not bleed. The knife stuck in my flesh leaves only the hole that proves I am dead.

Why does he write 'minor' martyrdoms? Didn't the crucifixion only last three days? Is it the shortness of the days of torture or the fact that hope still breathes that lets him say minor? How can anything so total not be major?

He has martyred me, but for no cause, nor has he any idea of the size and consequence of my wounds. Perhaps he will never know, for to say, You killed me daily and O most especially nightly, would imply blame. I do not blame, nor even say, You might have done this or this rather than that.

I even say, You must do that, you have to do it, there is no alternative, urging my own murder.

But if a knife is stuck in the engine that pumps my blood, my blood stops, no matter how I reason with it. Will he notice that my heart has ceased to beat?

But he may, O he may at one glance, restore me and

flood me with so much new love that every scar will have a satin covering and be new glitter to attack his heart. From this great distance, after these nights of separation, more I cannot see. My imagination is snowed under the eternal unpunctuated hours.

What should happen if there is no instantaneous resurrection, I do not know. Blackness worse than death's blackest premonitions, or the oblivion of the prehistoric tribes.

But of one thing I feel too deadly a foreboding: if ever again he lets those nights happen, or dallies with remorse for past sins to others while sinning most dangerously against me, I shall be unrevivable. I shall, whether I want to or not, be struck dead with the fact.

And he may clothe it in all humanity's most melting colours, and pity, and sympathy, and call on love to be kind, and I too shall pray, Let me be kind, but it will be no good. Only the fact has potency, and that fact will be fatal.

It is not possible that he will not return. I lie here 500 miles away, on one elbow, hourly expecting his light peremptory tap on the door. Each time the inefficient jangle of the elevator gets into motion I start up: Will, oh will, this monster disgorge my miracle? a telegram? a phone call?

This is the grass of hope that grows indomitably over my mind, which dares not admit that perhaps tonight his mouth, like the centre of all roses, closes over a mouth not mine, burrowing with apologies and love, like a baby at the breast.

For to say he will not and never come is to throw myself into the whirlpool and to deliver my mind into madness and my dear, my unborn child into a flood of blood and death. This I cannot do, and nature sends me a thousand desperate instincts which make me hurry up and down streets, scrutinize magazines, and become feverishly absorbed in the price of gramophones.

I will not think of the thing now. I have no time. When I have washed my stockings I will. When I have sewn on a button I will. When I have written a letter I will.

With precious meticulousness nature showers me with the skill of Penelope for small precise tasks I bungled before: button-hole making and frills for collars. For dear God I must not think now, for I cannot cry here. The walls are too thin.

There is nowhere and never a time for such a word.

I can do nothing, being paralyzed by doubt. I can only wait, like an egg for the twenty-first day, for him to arrive with all the west winds of irrefutable conviction. Doubt claws off the safety covering which I had laid over the past totem poles of danger and scars of his past woundings. Doubt like a Harpy claws off the smooth surfaces where death might lie concealed in deceit and withdrawal.

I am more vulnerable than the princess for whom seven mattresses could not conceal the pea. It is not the certainties which love cannot surmount, but the doubts the terrible doubts that make Vesuvius in my stomach. Doubt brings enough clues for me to finish the conundrum into damnation for myself.

O then, I stiffen into horror, and the 500 miles stand like armies between us, and I could rush to her in a thaw of remorse and shame to have killed her all for nothing.

O, I understand too well how we are all Lot's wife, looking back, under our heroic loving faces. But is nothing irrefutable? Is no fact impregnable? Is there no once-in-a-billion years' bull's-eye worth even the slaughter of decisive action?

Our passion by the ice pond forced the sun into sight. It has rocked orphans to sleep and thickened the heart of the new-made cabinboy. Heathcliff's look bored a hole through England which generations of heather on the wild moor never erased.

Give me my faith in the one fact, and I can cure cancer and gossip and war. Give me the fact, and then I would cut off my hands and give them to her to comfort her for an hour.

Injure me, betray me, but only make me sure of the love, for all day and all night, away from him and with him, everywhere and always, that is my gravity, and the apples (which ben ripe in my gardayne) fall only towards that.

Always on these nights that demand decision, the cold streets write the answer in the blood, the same that carves the wrinkles in the old women's faces: the wisdom old people get because they cannot remember the passion.

The young say, Why not die before such ignominy?

But the old trudge over Europe pushing carts and enormous bloated-with-hunger bellies, fight like cats for a crust to keep alive with, and are glad to find reward in a cake with pink icing.

Is it that they forget or that there is truly compensation in a long-off view?

Boys and middle-aged men put pistols to their temples, or jump from forty-storey windows for pride.

But the old are content to solicit a look from those who have usurped their place. Do they really see all? Or does nature walk beside them, holding their flabby forearms and whispering medicinal lies? For memory deserts them and their eyes get dimmer as the past achieves perspective. Who can say there is anything won at such a price?

'I think I see the world laid out like a corpse, my dear, but my eyes are old and I can't be sure.'

'Last night I heard a flock of angels crying outside my window, but it may not have been, my ears are not what they were. It's of no consequence. Don't trouble to find out.'

Will we have anything at all to say, we who already know too much? 'It doesn't matter really, it's all the same in the end.'

> 'If thou wilt ease thine heart
>   Of love and all its smart,
>   Then sleep, dear, sleep.'

O the fingers of the cold, the little creeping fingers of dissuasion.

PART NINE

The grass is already green in the country. My imagination clutches that fact like a hot-water bottle, and makes itself dopey with it, and uses it like a drug to ease my heart and quiet all my sources of unrest. My future is already planted there, and my hope getting ready to sprout with the cherry blossom.

My lover hovers around his murder. I cannot call him. I cannot say, Make the final kill, and neither can I say, Revive her and stay with her forever, the only alternative.

He is not here. He is all gone. There is only the bloated globe. Nothing but the bracelet he put around my wrist reminds me I was once alive. My dead eye and my blank days only prove I am dead, not why, not his existence.

I contemplate vaguely the instruments of love, and say with cold wonder, Did the world rock for his touch on the threshold of this? The breast that once caught fire from far away lies colder and less ignitable than Everest.

This state is far from longing because it is far beyond it. It is the state where the unbearable suffers eclipse and becomes coma. It is so much in the unremembering purgatorial state that I have no belief in revival, no real belief in the return of Spring, in love, in our joined mouths.

Was it ever like that? Did we lie so close like irresistible currents driven together?

If I had wit to remember that my present numbness comes expressly from my too intense love, all would be proved. But logic is not love's pageboy, and does not attend coma either.

How headlessly I drift. How dangerously uninhabited.

Sometimes I glimpse an awakening – but the nightmare of knowledge-too-late, like a volcano erupting in my imagination, brings back a thicker fog. Like the madman with his askew eyes glued to a bead, I see that cherry-tree and the green grass, and focus on it, and bend all in that direction. It will be achieved by the madman's meticulousness.

But tomorrow and tomorrow and tomorrow lie as locked and uncharted as the other face of the moon, and have far, far less curiosity concerning them. I reach the cherry-tree and we all blossom. Or I reach the tree and we die. But I reach the tree. That is my entire plan and all the goal for my remaining forty years, if, as seems impossible, so many remain.

By the Pacific I wander like Dido, hearing such a passion of tears in the breaking waves, that I wonder why the whole world isn't weeping inconsolably.

On the grass, under the pines, I sit up starkly, for even to recline reminds me of the stances of love, and I am unable to bear the pain of so much remembering. Then I wander uphill, contemplating my feet with a desperate fierce lack of all feeling, and I say, O is she too pressing her feet into the service of sedative monotony?

It is the dead moments when the beauty, though

smacked in the face, is unregistered, and unfelt, that I also know what she feels walking without her heart.

And what of my angel, her now lost angel, hanging fire between all the wars? He squirms in his inaction, is impotent for means, and pierced by the spring night that illegally enters New York.

Who were the female saints, I say, and how did they manage to fill their beds with God? How can any woman from this empty world construct communication with heaven? Then, sitting down on a stone with the lie of Wordsworth's life under my arm, I ask myself, What is love?, dissecting it in my most pedantic words, assuring myself that all that blood was spilt to make me a philosopher.

But all the while, like a new-made lighthouse keeper, scanning the sea for a boat bringing coloured periodicals and gossip, my soul is leaning ardently to catch the rustle of a letter bringing me a reprieve.

At night I walk the dusty road, calling the moonlight chaste and ecclesiastical, praying, lest I too much remember, that I become a hermit, that I strain forever upward, or descend in a shower of the spirit's blood.

Let me lie on the cold stones! Let me lift weights too heavy for me! Let me cry More! to pain, with a white face shaping through fire, with whips of endurance, with cords of the invulnerable ascetic, into the badge of the possible saint!

But my own feet blur the message the silence has for my ears, and at night my breast falls into my hand like a creature unbearable and unjustly abused.

But why elaborate? Say it so that the neighbours can understand: When we lie in bed I feel . . .

Don't you feel blue all by your lonesome?

Yes, I do, don't you.

Oh, and it's so cold in bed.

Which side did the good-looking blonde lie on? It gives me ideas.

The dogwood is dropping its ears. It is overpowered by summer. So is coquetry overpowered by procreancy. I grow too unwieldy to dance the minuet.

She's expecting another baby in the next six months.

Hm. Hm. Just as I thought.

As I was walking in a thick part of the wood I found a little grave. I thought it was a new flower, there were two primrose plants growing on it. Who waters her shame with tears by the decaying cedar trees?

I didn't like to ask anyone. They eye me. They bore a hole in my wedding finger because it is bare, and they measure my belly like tailors, to weave a juicy bit of gossip.

You're in a bad way, aren't you, my dear? You're in quite a spot?

Oh no, thank you, I'm all right, I'm fine. A little short of cash, maybe.

If there's anything you'd like to tell me, you can trust me, you know. I've been around, my husband and I, we've been around.

Oh no, thank you, I'm fine.

I don't like to say anything but it was rather queer, you know, the way you arrived and everything. You know how people will talk, and then you don't look more than a kid.

Oh, I'm old, I'm 23.

Really! I wouldn't have thought it. I'm 35. I have a bedroom suite *and* a parlour suite *and* lace doilies *and* a mahogany rack for magazines: we're ambitious, my husband and I.

I heard the neighbours' daughters talking: Under the moon, he! he! he! What were *you* doing parking in the bend in the road?

Oh! I'm not at all sexy, I get so bored necking, but I don't like to hurt their feelings. It's different with some of my girl-friends, you know, they have to have lots of self-control, you wouldn't believe it. I don't know what it is with me, I guess I'm just built that way.

Witches were burnt at the stake, all over New England, just for love, just for wearing the lineaments of gratified desire.

I am lonely. I cannot be a female saint. I want the one I want. He is the one I picked out from the world. I picked him out in cold deliberation. But the passion was not cold. It kindled me. It kindled the world. Love, love, give my heart ease, put your arms round me, give my heart ease. Feel the little bastard.

The small hard head juts out near my bladder. That's our child. That's the reward of love. That's why I drink milk and close my ears to the shock of disaster and the rage of gossips and the thunder of war. I listen to Mozart, I gather the spring flowers, wandering in the sun.

The child ejects calm, but he cannot dispel the loneliness. Time passes, but the loneliness grows greater than the child. It is more unwieldy.

O waste of moon, waste of lavish spring blossoms and lilac as I pass down the path. Cease all blandishments to squander them at his feet, to win him away to life, to be on my side. O be my allies, unfolding ferns, butterfly in the wood.

But relentless Spring goes on and dares to finish itself without him, and I grow from one shape into another, and the oblivious child leaps without waiting for a father.

Forty days in the wilderness and not one holy vision. Sights to dazzle the eye, but I bask in the sun without drawing one metaphor from it. Nature is using me. I am the seedbag. Jumping down rocks and hills I have a different balance, and fall backward or trip too easily, overloaded in front.

But I draw no parallels from patterns, and throw off no silver-sparkled words from my encounters. Pull down the blinds, my embryo, over my eyes.

But my eyes, like the bloody setting sun, peer through the veils and mists which rise from sorrow, towards that meeting which I must have or die. And, like a burst spring, my will, which had been labouring upward, uncoils with a frantic clatter. I am hurtled out of the meadow of calm, which nothing O nothing ever can make me believe in.

The next generation cannot dam my passion. No one can throw me a pulley. I must retrace my steps and embrace my sentence. I cannot live out of earshot of my doom, hoping to salvage something from the blood. I can salvage neither the Memory nor the Child. Love is my double or nothing.

Pain, pain that will bring me my son, step through the curtains of the officious housewife nature, and give me the truth first, or give me nothing. Nature for her embryo fights like her tigresses with all her weapons, but my mind is sharp with pain, and gimlets a hole through natural salvation.

My feet down the wet street hurry to catch the train, and my hand clutches my ticket to damnation. Bow down thou tall cherry-tree, I am going to meet my lover.

No ounce of consolation if this fails. No resurrection and no after-life. I have tried the remedies and they have all failed. Despair grows like a weed to hope. Despair grows, and like the cuckoo bird ousts my sleeping baby. Perhaps, perhaps, but I can wait no longer.

Fate, receive my final ultimatum, delivered by me, and signed this day with my hand, signed and well and truly considered, my last and unchangeable will.

PART TEN

By Grand Central Station I sat down and wept:

I will *not* be placated by the mechanical motions of existence, nor find consolation in the solicitude of waiters who notice my devastated face. Sleep tries to seduce me by promising a more reasonable tomorrow. But I will not be betrayed by such a Judas of fallacy: it betrays everyone: it leads them into death. Everyone acquiesces: everyone compromises.

They say, As we grow older we embrace resignation.

But O, they totter into it blind and unprotesting. And from their sin, the sin of accepting such a pimp to death, there is no redemption. It is the sin of damnation.

But what except morphine can weave bearable nets around the tigershark that tears my mind to shreds, seeking escape on every impossible side? The senses deliver the unbearable into sleep, and it ceases, except that it appears gruesomely at the edges of my dreams, making ghastly signals which wear away peace, but which I cannot understand.

The pain was unbearable, but I did not want it to end: it had operatic grandeur. It lit up Grand Central Station like a Judgment Day. It was more iron-muscled than

Samson in his moment of revelation. It might have shown me all Dante's dream. But there was no way to endure.

I am going to have a child, so all my dreams are of water, across which the ghost of an almost accomplished calamity beckons. But tonight that child lay within like the fated and only island in all seas.

When Lexington Avenue dissolved in my tears, and the houses and the neon lights and the nebulæ fell jumbled into the flood, that child was the naked newborn babe striding the blast. He is the one focal pinning me to my own centre.

But the sea that floods is love, and it gushes out of me like an arterial wound. I am drowning in it. The fifty-storey windows glitter and collapse into water. The water is all full of astronomical points. It is a magnetic deathtrap. Everything is caught in its rush.

Where are we all headed for on the swollen river of my undammed grief? O hurricane, be decisive. Terminate in any end, but terminate.

The grief trumpets its triumph. It is raving. It craves violence for expression, but can find none. There is no end. The drowning never ceases. The water submerges and blends, but I am not dead. O I am not dead. I am under the sea. The entire sea is on top of me.

Then I speed through Grand Central Station with nothing at all to stop me, like a careering limousine without brakes, propelled by my brilliant desperation.

It gives me talent. It manipulates the small terrorizers of before. I storm them with scorn.

Go to Hell! I say to the ones that used to cow me when I humbly asked for a sandwich.

They obey the glint in the middle of my glazed eye, for it is the fierce last stand of all I have. I cannot now invoke bows and ubiquitous smiles for there is twelve cents left of that unfailing bribery, and my face floated away on that hæmorrhage of sorrow that dissolved even the chromium-plating the glass palaces the concrete of New York.

But these all-night cafés see too much of the derelict who warms himself with coffee before throwing himself into the river. These tables are topped in leather on which the blood has never dried. They invite one to compose farewell notes: 'Goodbye All – I couldn't take it.'

'She had a distracted air,' they tell the police, 'But then we get so many of her kind. It's all in the night's work.'

They shake their heads as they watch her go, whisking away the empty coffee-cup: 'Someone done her wrong,' they gag, protecting themselves against the ultimate terror with the ghost-proof joke. 'Tough – Well, Ma'am, what'll it be?'

I race disaster down Third Avenue. It shimmers in the Hudson River. When I dare to look up for a sign of comfort the neons flash relentlessly.

No, no one will pity you here where failure is the same as shame, and tears anachronisms, out of place even in cinemas.

'Sure, kid. We all got troubles. Buck up. Take it on the chin.'

If you can smile now you might become a great success in the advertising business. Brave little woman . . . Quite a gal. Her saucy repartee conceals alluring tragedy. Once she could feel, she could weep. Once she too was human. But you see what can be done? Why, she's making $15,000 a year.

Somebody is in the temple, God, and they're doling out phoney dollar bills. I didn't ask for them to envy me, or even for shoes in the fashionable shade. I wanted only one thing. I gave you the full instructions. The name, I spelt it out in letters as long as a continent, even the address, the address that makes waterfalls of my blood because it is also her address.

I said quite plainly and loudly: This is what I want. I want this, and I don't want any bonus. Just give me this and I'll pay any price you ask. I made no reservations. You took advantage of this. I never grudged. But, Sir, so what I plead is just – what are you stalling for? There is no more to give.

The bus conductor covers his ham sandwich with mustard, standing up, all in a hurry between cars. He has come and gone while I put three crosses on my grave. When will you have time for love, sweetheart?

It sits like his ham sandwich in a small knot in his stomach. 'If you are in a hurry, try Tums for indigestion. Tums are tops for those on the run.'

Punctually, like his ticket-puncher, he goes in and out of the cave of revelation. One eye is full of dust from the street and the other is on the clock. Wife, open your legs. Five minutes and I go on duty.

I see her often, battling for bargain stockings in

Macy's basement. Who will untwist the petrified growth of her face? Who will cut this very Gordian knot?

Sheers, O you mad frivolous Sisters, sheers.

My love is crucified on a floating cross, and cries out hoarsely my name in the night. His wife hears and her eyes burn holes in the darkness across the room. My love has a bandage like a bowel of pain around his neck, where lately he cut his throat.

But it is not the wound that chokes him every time he swallows. It is the ball of the world, spiked where Europe is, but covered like a tea-cosy with my name. O how thirsty he is when that great globe closes his throat.

He hangs, damp with his impotent tears, nailed by one hand to Love and by the other one to Pity, with his two feet nailed to the longitude of the inevitable, floating in the perpetual seas of tragedy, in the gales of these special times.

All my polestars have become falling stars. My mind floats like flotsam on the general flood. No morbid adolescent ever clutched toward melodramatic conclusion so wildly. The world goes roaring up.

Oh yes, it is hysteria that whips me with his name, that drives me with the insane loneliness of the first split amœba, to shriek beneath his window. As if all future worlds lay in the conjunction of our separated cells, I writhe in desperation, screaming his name, as my germ dwindles, as the whole universe withers, like a corolla no bee ever found.

★ ★ ★

He still tosses. Though sleeping, he is on the rack.

Across the room she lies livid with grief and love, legendary and stony as a Catholic Cathedral.

This one was the perfect sacrifice. All civilized men will weep for her. Choirs will mourn forever in front of that legitimate, moving memorial. Their disciplined tears will grow grass so green it touches untouched hearts.

Every brick was blood. The spire gored her for christening, even while her upturned face expected the kiss of Christ. The stones are smooth because her agony rolled them out. She was spilt as offering. Three times she was martyred, but the third time she truly died.

He stands paralyzed, watching her hang. Her dying eye rolls round and sees how her god betrays her. But she murmurs, 'In la sua voluntade . . .'

Harlots have eyes that scamper like mice round restaurants dotted with haphazard prospects. Their clattery laughter lullabies trouble like the wooden cradle on the floor. My cradle is within. It rocks, but a hurricane rocks it. Its elbows bleed me. It buffets me off the road of planned elegance. Girls in love, remember to keep your heads, keep calm, plan your campaign, yours sincerely, Dorothy Dix. Girls in love, be harlots, it hurts less.

He rocks also in his trapezist's net, hung in a hurricane, but hung above damnation. O hurricane, be decisive, terminate in any end, but terminate.

How can I pity him even though he lies so vulnerable up there in the stinging winds, when every hole that bleeds me was made by a kiss of his? He is beautiful as allegory. He is beautiful as the legend the imagination washes up on the sand.

But what bombards him except the indiscriminate elements, chancy as lightning, ubiquitous as air? He is open to a thousand cries of distraction and terror. He swings delirious in the night, shuddering and fighting off a thousand foes and woes.

But O my burning baby anchors love within me, and I am consumed wherever I go, like a Saint Catherine's wheel of torture, perpetual as the turning earth, and far less likely to go out.

In a day or two the tempest will abate, dear heart, dear Catherine. Be calm, be kind.

In an hour, my angel of pain, a comet has dashed its perpetuity against eternal calamity.

O, calamity is the waiter brushing the crumbs from the red leather table, grinning with his gold teeth, to boast later to the boys.

There is no tomorrow, not reason's nor any other. And today, my only today, I spill uselessly into my ten-cent notebook, my eyes used up with tears. This is the hour I once rose up, and beautifully equipped with scorn, commanded the sun to rise. Now this is no hour and it leads nowhere. It dangles meaninglessly.

Who shuffles by me gripping chairs for support? I do. I myself. I reel round the café, solicited by the prostitute sleep. Every tear is wept and lies staining its falling place. I am without words. I am without thoughts. But quia amore langueo. I am dying for love. This is the language of love.

Tomorrow at ten I shall take a train. All trains lead me to rivers that beckon and wink. Through the day, or through the twilight, I rush past rivers to *the* river. One river waits. One is the one, and knows how I shall fall into the water with a thud.

And I am drenched before I reach the surface. I am drowned before I reach the waterweeds at the bottom. I avoid the glance the river gives me. But it dances on. It has lust for me. I am almost succumbed.

In my dreams of most terror, the water freezes into ice, the waterfall that promises liberation stands stock-still and disobedient. I am baulked then, like a man coffined alive, or a chained ghost never to be let loose.

His hand of sympathy goes out to me, soft as a dove, his cheek like early apples. He weeps consolation on my mouth. He kisses the circles on top of the water beneath which I lie drowned. Soft as a fish, the kiss glides down to me, it swims through me, trailing its bubbles of love. All the ton pressures of all the oceans cannot withstand that touch that prods me with regret.

Through the layers of impenetrability, Tomorrow, like an ardent boy of Socrates, looks down at the drowned with resurrection in his eyeballs. I see my lover's limbs all intertwined with his. My lover is making signs. He smiles. He points. He stoops down his hand into the water and destroys my image with ripples. The mud covers me up. The mud puts curtains over my eyes. My cries now rise back in bubbles, my screams only prick the air like dragonfly's messages.

Then the confusion clears. I see it is a summer's evening above. My lover lies under the linden-tree kissing Tomorrow with his mouth that was all mine. O the tumult, the unavailing ineffectual uproar of the damned. O the language of love. The uninterpreted. The inarticulate. Amore. Amore. Amore.

★ ★ ★

Is it possible he cannot hear me when he lies so close, so lightly asleep? These hours are the only hours. What can sleep give him to compare with what I could have given him? He must start up. He must come here and find me.

He cries out in his sleep. He sees the huge bird of catastrophe fly by. Both its wings are lined with the daily paper. Five million other voices are shrieking too. How shall I be heard?

'Lie still, my dear,' his guardian angel says.

'Is everything all right?'

'No, but lie still all the same.'

Dawn creeps over his window like a guilty animal. This is the very room he chose instead of love. Let it be quiet and full of healing. For me it blocks all vision, all perspective. It is the cursed comfort he preferred to my breast.

The one who shares it weeps silently in corners, is tender unnoticed, and makes his necessary tea.

'Have you seen my notebook, dear?'

'It is under the desk, my sweet.'

Give it to him, O my gentle usurper, whom I also have usurped, my enemy whom I have both killed and been killed by. Let him write words that will acquit him of these murders.

The page is as white as my face after a night of weeping. It is as sterile as my devastated mind. All martyrdoms are in vain. He also is drowning in the blood of too much sacrifice.

Lay aside the weapons, love, for all battles are lost.

★ ★ ★

And what will the rose and the briar tell my sister's children playing near the grave? It pricks my hand, the pretty flower. Of a rose is all my song.

But what did they kill each other for? How should I know, my little Wilhelmine? It is the language of love, which nobody understands. It is the first cry of my never-to-be-born child. Go into your garden, for your apples are ripe.

Like the genii at hell's gates, the darkie porters arrive, and usher in the day with brooms and enormous dustpans. Odours of disinfectant wipe out love and tears. With rush and thunder the early workers overrun the world they have inherited, tramping out the stains of the wailing, bleeding past.

'Goodmorning, Boss. A cup of coffee and two fried eggs.'

Look at the idiot boy you begot with that night. He is all the world that is left. He is America, and better than love. He is civilization's heir, O you mob, whose actions brought him into being.

He is happier than you, sweetheart. But will he do to fill in these coming thousand years? Well, it's too late now to complain, my honey-dove. Yes, it's all over. No regrets. No postmortems. You must adjust yourself to conditions as they are, that's all. You have to learn to be adaptable.

I myself prefer Boulder Dam to Chartres Cathedral. I prefer dogs to children. I prefer corncobs to the genitals of the male. Everything's hotsy-totsy, dandy, everything's OK. It's in the bag. It can't miss.

My dear, my darling, do you hear me where you sleep?